# Betrayed 3:

## Camaiyah's Redemption

### TANISHA STEWART

**Betrayed 3: Camaiyah's Redemption**

Copyright © 2019 Tanisha Stewart

All rights reserved.

Books may be purchased in quantity and for special sales by contacting the publisher, Tanisha Stewart, by email at tanishastewart.author@gmail.com.

Cover Design: Tanisha Stewart
http://www.tanishastewartauthor.com

Editing: Janet Angelo
https://indiegopublishing.com/
First Edition

Published in the United States of America by Tanisha Stewart

# Table of Contents

# To the Reader

If you enjoy this quick read, please know that I appreciate so much a positive review on Amazon.

Also, if you would like to read more of my work, or hear more about me as an author, feel free to join my reader's group on Facebook: <u>Tanisha Stewart Readers</u>, or my email list at https://www.tanishastewartauthor.com/contact, or follow me on social media:

Facebook: Tanisha Stewart, Author
Instagram: tanishastewart_author
Twitter: TStewart_Author

# Betrayed 3:

## Camaiyah's Redemption

# Chapter 1

Camaiyah pulled out of the parking lot of R&R Spa, where she had been working as a masseuse for the past five years. She was so tired and burned out. "I need a drink," she muttered with a sigh. She turned down a side street to the package store in search of some liquid comforts.

Today marked six months since she, June, and Iliana broke off their friendship. She hated to admit it, even to herself, but she kind of missed them – well, at least Iliana. She had stopped liking June a long time ago.

She sucked her teeth when she saw that nearly every space was taken in the parking lot of the liquor store. "I'm just trying to get in and out today!" She yelled at the world through clenched teeth. "And nobody better try to holla either."

She quickly pulled into a space way at the end after someone else pulled out of it. Another driver who had been eyeing the spot from the opposite direction threw up her hands in frustration.

"Bitch, I know you ain't taking my spot!" the other woman yelled through her open window as she drove at a crawl past Camaiyah's car to circle around and hunt for a new spot.

Camaiyah cocked her head out her window. "Yes I am! And?"

Most girls were scared of her because of her size, and the ones that weren't quickly learned to be afraid after catching those hands. Camaiyah often described herself as thick but proportional.

She sauntered to the door of the establishment, making sure she shot a final glance at that other driver before she walked in. "Hmph," she muttered, noticing that the woman was idling near Camaiyah's car as she waited for an empty space.

As soon as Camaiyah entered the store, she could feel all eyes on her. It was packed with men of all shapes and sizes. Unfortunately, only the older, fat, balding ones decided to give her any verbal attention.

"Hey, lil baby," said a toothless one, staring directly at her behind. "Why don't you let me take you out tonight?"

Camaiyah curled her lip at him in disgust. Her eyes and attitude said, *Let me hurry up and get the hell out of here.* She walked as far away from him as she could, which was hard to do in such a small store. She eyed the selections then quickly grabbed a bottle of Henny, her go-to after a long, stressful day.

When she got in line, the toothless old man was still in the same spot, staring at her. He immediately cut back into the conversation as if she never left.

"So what you think about that?" He licked his lips.

Camaiyah fought her urge to vomit as she focused on the back of the t-shirt of the man standing in front of her. *All these damn men in here, and nobody even comes to my rescue.*

"Hey," he said again, then had the nerve to touch her to get her attention. "I'm talking to you."

*This nigga did* not *just try to put some bass in his voice!* She mustered up as defiant a look as possible, but at the same time, she was feeling kind of nervous.

"Hey, man," said the cashier, noticing what was going on. "If you not going to buy anything, you gotta leave."

Camaiyah shot him a look of gratitude. He responded with a smile.

The old man looked up at him then back at Camaiyah.

"Fine." He shuffled his way out of the store.

"Thank God," she breathed, and the line moved forward.

\*\*\*

Later on that night, Camaiyah was scrolling her timeline. She had finished about half her bottle of Henny and was feeling kind of good. She checked to see how many likes she had on her new profile picture, and exactly who had liked it. There were a few cute guys, but her eyes rolled when she saw that Kay'Ceon, her ex fling and June's ex boyfriend, had loved it.

As if he knew she was looking at it right then, a comment from him popped up under her photo.

*Lookin good, girl.*

It freaked her out at first, and then it annoyed her. She sucked her teeth. "I told his ass I wasn't interested." The alcohol told her to write a nasty response, but her right mind told her to let it go.

She went to Iliana's page. She had been thinking about her earlier after she got off work. "I wonder what she been up to," she murmured. She scrolled down and saw a bunch of selfies of Iliana and Kelvin together.

She sucked her teeth again, but then her heart panged as she realized that even Iliana's awkward ass could get a man, and here she was with no one. She almost liked one of their pictures, which was actually kind of cute. Iliana and Kelvin had gone on a hiking trip and taken a selfie at the top of the mountain with a panoramic view behind them. It was a really romantic photo.

"Girl, that's just the liquor talking," she said under her breath. She scrolled down a little more but stopped when she saw another photo with Iliana, Kelvin, Coop, and June. It looked like they had gone out on a double date to Dave and Busters and had a good time.

"She doesn't even belong with him!" Camaiyah spat, referring to June. She was still highly irritated over the fact that June was going steady with her cousin.

Camaiyah closed out of the app before her anger took over. "Time to take my ass to bed."

*** 

Camaiyah had the next day off, so she decided to head to Coop's gym. She wasn't the

5

working out type, but she had gotten a membership to support her cousin's endeavor, and also to possibly hook up with someone worthwhile. So far, all the dudes seemed to be interested in the skinny broads, but Camaiyah held out hope that someone would notice her.

As she made her way to the treadmills, she saw that a cardio class was about to start. "Hmmm...maybe I do need to work up a sweat." She entered the room and quickly grabbed a spot next to a girl of average build, the kind of person who looked like she would have to put some effort into her workout. *Good, I won't feel so big next to her.*

"Hey," said the girl, and gave her a friendly half smile.

"Hey," Camaiyah said, and smiled back before focusing on the instructor.

"Okay, let's get started, everybody!" The instructor, a woman who looked a few years older than Camaiyah, was a little too upbeat for Camaiyah's liking, but she clearly must have known what she was doing based on her six-pack abs, so Camaiyah decided to stick around and endure her exuberance.

The class started with a warm-up, which was pretty easy, though Camaiyah could definitely feel herself working up a sweat already.

By the time they were about five minutes in, things got more intense. Camaiyah felt like she had made a mistake by joining in. She was barely able to keep up with all the jumps, squats, and lunges, and she was literally huffing for breath. At first she felt like she was the only one struggling, but then she noticed that the girl next to her was doing worse than she was, so she resolved to at least do better than her for the duration of the workout.

By the time the thirty-minute session was over, Camaiyah was drenched in sweat. "Never again," she said on a long exhale, though she actually felt kind of good.

"I know that's right," said the girl, panting for breath.

Camaiyah shot her a glance.

"I'm Ce'Anna." She smiled.

"Camaiyah," she responded, deciding it wouldn't hurt to return the friendliness.

The girls walked together to the locker room to freshen up.

"So how long have you been a member?" said Ce'Anna after splashing her face with some water. She wiped it with a towel.

"I joined when it opened," said Camaiyah. "My cousin is one of the owners."

"Really?" Ce'Anna looked at her in the mirror. "That's great!"

They made their way back into the gym just as Coop walked through the front doors. "That's him right there." Camaiyah gestured toward him. "Hey cuz!" she said, and they hugged. "We still on for tonight?"

"Sure," he smiled then looked at Ce'Anna.

"This is Ce'Anna," Camaiyah said, not missing a beat. "She just took the cardio class with me."

"Oh really?" Coop said. "How was it?"

"It was hard, but I enjoyed it."

"Me too," said Ce'Anna. She gazed at Coop then broke eye contact out of nervous attraction.

*She's feeling him*, Camaiyah observed. *This could be good.*

"Well, I won't hold you ladies," said Coop. "I have a meeting. I'll see you later, Camaiyah."

They watched him walk away.

"I imagine a lot of females join this gym," Ce'Anna remarked, staring a little too long at his broad shoulders and backside.

The wheels were already turning for Camaiyah. "Indeed they do."

***

Later on that night, Camaiyah and Coop were watching movies at her apartment. Despite the fact that he had hooked up with June,

8

Camaiyah really loved having her cousin around again.

"This is crazy," Camaiyah said after a particularly riveting scene in the latest *Fast and Furious* movie.

"Right," said Coop. "I need a whip like that." He stuffed another handful of popcorn into his mouth, and right then, his phone rang. He placed his popcorn bowl on the coffee table and grabbed his phone.

"One second, I gotta get this." He hopped up and went to the kitchen.

Camaiyah rolled her eyes and paused the movie. *Must be June on the phone, Little Miss Precious Perfect.* If it was Vel or Drew, his business partners, he would have stayed in the living room.

Camaiyah impatiently scrolled her timeline until Coop returned.

"Is she gonna be calling you all night?" she snapped when he came back into the living room.

Coop shot her a pained look. "Camaiyah, why you tripping?"

"I'm not tripping. Why does she have to be all up under you? She knows you're over here, right?"

Coop sighed. "Can we just get back to the movie, please?"

9

"Yeah, as long as she doesn't keep blowing up your phone."

Coop looked like he'd had enough. "Look Camaiyah, I don't understand how you can't stand her so much. Wasn't y'all best friends since like kindergarten?"

"I been stopped liking her."

"So why did you continue to be friends with her for all those years? I never knew you to be fake."

Camaiyah's ears grew hot. "Nobody was being fake. It's just—"

"Just what?" Coop crossed his arms.

Camaiyah paused. "Let's get back to the movie."

She pressed play before he could say anything else, but his words stuck with her through the rest of the movie, and long after he left for the night.

*Was I being fake?*

# Chapter 2

The morning sun filtered through the blinds in Ce'Anna and Camron's bedroom, waking her up. She groaned and rolled over, and lay there a few minutes more to convince herself to get up to go to the bathroom. It had been two days since the cardio class, but her legs still felt like they could barely move after all those squats and lunges. "I really need to get back in shape," she muttered. She yawned, stretched, and made herself trudge to the bathroom.

When she came back into the bedroom, Camron was still snoring. She decided to let him sleep a little longer.

"I might as well make breakfast." She grabbed her robe from the back of the bedroom door and made her way to the kitchen. Even though it had been three years, it seemed like just yesterday that she had been in the kitchen cooking breakfast for Trent.

Their divorce still pained her, though it had long been finalized. Her lost friendship with her two besties, Natasha and Rachel, also still deeply affected her.

But two very good things had come into her life after her divorce from Trent: her son, Trent Junior, and her new husband, Camron.

She hummed as she entered the kitchen and turned on the radio they kept on the counter. She found an upbeat station and got busy cooking.

Soon, the house was filled with the delicious aromas of pancakes, sausage, and grits with cheddar cheese.

"Hoo-wee, girl!" said Camron as he entered the kitchen wearing his robe. "I knew I put it on you last night, but I didn't know it was like that!"

He wrapped his arms around Ce'Anna from behind and kissed her neck as she stood at the stove fixing their plates.

"Boy, stop," she mock scolded with a teasing grin. "You know I cook every Saturday."

He took his seat at the breakfast table as she set his plate and utensils in front of him then went to get her own. He poured himself some orange juice from the pitcher she had put on the table, then filled Ce'Anna's glass.

"Thanks, babe." She took a bite of sausage. "Oh, man, this is good, if I don't say so myself."

"You know it." Camron dug into his cheese grits. "So, little man staying with Trent for the whole weekend?"

A dark look crossed Ce'Anna's face for a split second. She couldn't stand Trent's wife being around her son. "Yeah, and he's bringing him to daycare on Monday as well. We'll pick him up on our way home."

She and Camron taught at the same elementary school, which was kind of awkward at times, but also beneficial, because it saved gas and mileage.

"Maybe we can try for a little one of our own soon," Camron said.

Ce'Anna tensed. She had been dreading this conversation, though she knew it was coming. It was almost like déjà vu. When she and Trent were married, he had pressured her to have a child.

"Right, maybe one day soon." She hoped her fake agreement was enough to keep him at bay for a while.

She allowed her mind to wander as she and Camron ate the rest of their breakfast in silence. *I wonder what Trent's doing right now?* She mused inwardly. When Camron abruptly pushed his chair back to get up from the table, she startled. "I gotta get over him," she muttered.

"What was that?" Camron said, raising his eyebrow at her as he reached for her empty plate.

She shook her head. "Nothing... I was just thinking about the lesson I have planned for Monday."

He smiled in response. "Always on the job."

"Always." She got up and went back to their bedroom to get ready for the day while Camron washed the dishes.

\*\*\*

Camron decided to spend that Saturday with his boys, so Ce'Anna went to the mall for some spa treatments. She got her nails and feet done first, and then she decided to get a massage before getting her hair done. She walked into R&R Spa, and almost breathed a sigh of relief at the calming atmosphere. It was her first time at this spa, and already she liked the ambience better than the one she usually went to.

She was greeted as soon as she walked in, and luckily, they had an immediate opening because another client had cancelled on one of their masseuses.

Ce'Anna's eyes widened when she saw that her masseuse was Camaiyah, the girl she had met at the gym.

"Hey!" she exclaimed. "I didn't know you worked here."

"Hey." Camaiyah's expression was unreadable at first, then she smiled. "I guess I'll be taking care of you today."

Ce'Anna followed Camaiyah to one of the back rooms, where she changed into the robe Camaiyah supplied her before they entered the massage room. She lay face down on the massage table.

Camaiyah knocked on the door. "All set?"

"Yup!"

Camaiyah entered then closed the door behind her and dimmed the lights. She turned on some soothing instrumental music.

"So, you signed up for a sixty-minute full body massage today, correct?" Her tone was so professional that she sounded like a different person. Ce'Anna almost looked up to see if someone else had taken Camaiyah's place.

"Yes, thank you."

"Okay, I just wanted to verify before we began."

Camaiyah explained to her the various pressure points she was going to hit, and let her know that if anything felt uncomfortable, she was free to speak up. Ce'Anna consented, and the massage began.

They made small talk at first, but then Ce'Anna felt herself drifting off to sleep as she became more and more comfortable. She closed her eyes for what felt like a minute, then she was awakened by Camaiyah gently nudging her.

Ce'Anna popped her head up. "What? Did I fall asleep? Oh, wow!"

Camaiyah smiled. "You must have been very comfortable."

Ce'Anna blushed. "I've never fallen asleep during a massage before. Usually, I would be too afraid to."

Camaiyah's smile widened as she finally broke her professional tone. "Guess I got the magic touch."

"Girl, you do indeed. After that brutal cardio workout the other night, my body has really needed this."

Ce'Anna changed into her clothes then paid at the front desk, making sure to give Camaiyah a huge tip. She went back out into the busy mall to get her hair done.

After her hair was styled, she was ready to go home. She began the long trek to the opposite end of the mall where her car was parked when she saw someone she never expected to see on a random Saturday like today. She stood still and watched as he approached, trying not to look too happy to see him, but she could feel herself smiling.

"Wow, hey!" she said, sounding a bit too eager before she could stop herself.

It had been almost three years since she had seen Xaveon in person, but he looked even better than he did when they were fooling around. His dreads were freshly twisted and cascading down his back.

He looked her up and down. "Ce'Anna."

"How have you been?" she said.

"Maintaining."

"Are you still with Natasha?" She just had to ask because, details.

He snorted. "That been over."

"Anybody new?"

"None of your concern."

She could tell he was irritated, but she persisted. "Listen, why don't we chat sometimes? We can still be friends." She reached out toward him, but he stepped away from her hand.

"I told you before we even started messing around that I don't do married chicks. You lied to me."

Underneath his cold exterior, Ce'Anna could sense that he was hurt. *Wow. I never knew. I thought it was just sex for him.*

She swallowed. "I'm sorry."

"Yeah."

Her demeanor shifted. "I mean, but we were both at fault though."

"Look, I'm not here to go back and forth with you. That situation been dead for a while. I'm just trying to have a pleasant Saturday afternoon at the mall. I didn't plan to run into you. I'm on my way somewhere else now, so I don't really have time to stand around and talk about the past. It's over and done with."

He stepped around her and continued on his way. Ce'Anna turned to watch him, wishing she had something to say that would make him come back and talk to her.

\*\*\*

That Wednesday was Parent Night at the daycare Trent Junior attended, and Camron said he wouldn't be able to make it because he felt like he was coming down with something, so Ce'Anna took extra time to make sure her hair looked perfect. Trent was planning to attend, and Ce'Anna wanted to look good in front of him even if she was his ex-wife.

She put on her red lipstick, the kind he always liked, and dressed in the sexiest outfit she could get away with for a school event, and spritzed herself liberally with his favorite perfume.

She kissed Camron goodbye and handed him his soup, and hurried out the door before he could ask why she'd made such an effort with her appearance just to attend a preschool parents' night.

When she and Trent Junior got there, they made their way to the cafeteria where the event was being held.

Ce'Anna's eyes scanned the room, then her heart stopped, and her smile turned into a frown when she saw Melissa, Trent's wife, making her way toward them.

"Hey, Ce'Anna!" Melissa threw her arms around Ce'Anna, hugging her before she could protest. Melissa never seemed to notice that Ce'Anna couldn't stand her.

"Hey," Ce'Anna responded, tucking a strand of her neatly pressed hair behind her ear that Melissa had dislodged with her exuberant hug. "Where's Trent?"

Melissa's eyes widened as she covered her mouth. "Oh, we forgot to call you! Trent couldn't make it tonight. He had to stay late in the office, but I was more than happy to stand in for him. Hey, little buddy!" She smiled down at Trent Junior holding Ce'Anna's hand.

"Missa!" He beamed up at her.

"It's so cute how he butchers my name." She smiled at Ce'Anna then touched his little cheek. "He's such a sweet little boy."

Ce'Anna fought back the urge to say, *Get your fucking hands off my son, bitch!* Instead, she smiled and offered a bland, "Yeah."

The mood, or at least Ce'Anna's mood, considerably soured as the night wore on. She kept a fake smile plastered on her face as she and Melissa greeted the other parents and their children, and she even managed to sit through the brief meeting with Trent Junior's teacher to learn about his progress. She felt conspicuous the whole time in her over-the-top outfit compared to the other women, who looked dowdy and rumpled, as if they'd come straight from work and hadn't had time to change. She caught more than a few stares, admiring glances from the men and dagger eyes from some of the women.

By the time the night was over, she and Trent Junior were exhausted, but for entirely different reasons.

# Chapter 3

Camaiyah went to visit her aunt Karyn.
They hadn't seen each other in over a week,
which was unusual. Aunt Karyn was Coop's
mother and Camaiyah's favorite aunt because
she always told it like it was.

"Hey, Auntie!" Camaiyah said as she
crossed the threshold into the house. She and
Aunt Karyn hugged.

"Girl, where you been at?" Aunt Karyn gave
her a once over.

"You know, just working and stuff."

Aunt Karyn pursed her lips. "And stuff,
huh?" She used air quotes to emphasize the
word stuff.

Camaiyah felt uneasiness building in her stomach. *Where is she going with this?* She shrugged. "I ain't been doing nothing out of the ordinary. Just working."

"Hmph."

"What have you been up to?" Camaiyah placed her hand on her hip, feigning attitude.

"Mm mm, honey. Don't get brand new." Aunt Karyn pointed her finger up and down at Camaiyah as she spoke. Then her expression changed. "I have been trying to figure out why you just can't seem to get along with my future daughter-in-law."

There it was. Camaiyah knew this was coming. "Auntie...." She sighed and walked over to the couch where she settled herself against the comfortable cushions at one end. "I did not come over here to talk about that girl."

Aunt Karyn sat at the other end of the couch. "That girl is the woman that Coop is in love with. You are going to have to find a way to get over that."

Camaiyah's eyes rolled almost involuntarily. "I don't know why he is with her in the first place."

"Why not?" Aunt Karyn countered. "She's a good girl, headed in the right direction in life. What's the problem?"

Camaiyah snorted in response. *What's* not *the problem?*

"You were her best friend for years. What led you to do what you did?"

Camaiyah felt herself growing hot under the collar. "Can we talk about something else?"

"Are you jealous?" Aunt Karyn stared her straight in the eyes, and her question sounded more like a statement than anything.

Camaiyah looked away. "Why would I be jealous?"

Aunt Karyn leaned across the sofa and gently cupped Camaiyah's cheek and turned her head so she was facing her again. "I think you are jealous, and I think you need to find out why."

\*\*\*

The next day, Camaiyah decided to take the cardio class again, despite the protests from her body. *I just need to drop a couple of pounds,* she reasoned as she purposely strode through the front doors of the building ready to do this thing. She took a glance into the room and saw that Ce'Anna wasn't there. "Thank God," she murmured, then she saw Coop exiting his office.

"Hey," she called out as she approached him.

"Hey." He looked uneasy.

Before Camaiyah could say another word, June emerged from Coop's office.

Camaiyah's eyes narrowed. "What are *you* doing here?"

June returned her steady gaze, hand on hip. "I was in my man's office, talking to him. What's it to you?"

"Don't try to act froggish cuz you think you got protection," Camaiyah countered.

Coop was so tired of this drama, every time they saw each other. "Ladies, can we please not—"

"I don't need protection," June retorted, "especially since I still owe you one for catfishing me."

"It's not my fault you can't tell fantasy from reality." That was a low blow, and Camaiyah knew it, but she didn't care.

June's face flushed. "Oh yeah? Well, it looks like my fantasy became a reality, and a mighty fine one at that." She slid her arm around Coop's and laced her fingers through his. "Where's your fantasy?"

Camaiyah's face twitched, and June took that as a sign of weakness, so she went in for the kill. "Or better yet, where's your reality?"

Camaiyah lunged, but Coop blocked it. "Camaiyah, chill. This is a place of business." His eyes pleaded, and that was the only thing that kept Camaiyah from unleashing her rage.

"Whatever," she shrugged, and glared at June. "If I see you on the streets, I got something for your ass."

Coop just shook his head, and June didn't acknowledge the threat. She and Coop walked hand-in-hand out of the gym and left Camaiyah standing there fuming.

*** 

Ce'Anna was running late to her cardio class, but she entered the gym just in time to see the heated exchange between Camaiyah, some other woman, and the sexy owner of the gym, Jermaine Cooper. Ce'Anna blushed when she thought of how thoroughly she'd looked him up online after Camaiyah introduced them after the last cardio class.

When June and Jermaine walked past her, she shot Jermaine a smile, but he didn't see it, and then she saw that he and this other woman were holding hands, and she felt ridiculous.

Camaiyah hesitated at the door to the cardio class, contemplating whether she should go in, and then she visibly took a deep breath and found an empty spot in the room.

Ce'Anna quickly followed her in.

"Hey, girl, what was that?" Ce'Anna said, gesturing to the lobby.

Camaiyah startled when she realized Ce'Anna was right there next to her. "What was what?"

"It looked like you were arguing with that woman."

Camaiyah snorted. "That bitch don't want it with me."

"Who is she?"

"Coop's girlfriend."

Ce'Anna's face fell. "Oh."

Camaiyah stared at her. "He needs to break up with her. She's no good for him."

*Well, I can think of a few things that would be good for him.* Ce'Anna fought to maintain a straight face. "Yeah, guys nowadays don't know a good woman from a bad one."

"Hmph. Tell me about it."

The instructor entered with her usual bubbly attitude. Ce'Anna glanced at Camaiyah again. "You ready for this class?"

"Yup," Camaiyah said, but it looked like she was speaking more to herself than to Ce'Anna.

\*\*\*

The class seemed like it was more exerting than the first one Ce'Anna took. *Maybe they jack up the intensity each time,* she mused, wiping sweat from her forehead. When it was finally over, she and Camaiyah exchanged numbers and agreed to go out for lunch some time.

Ce'Anna wanted nothing more than a shower and a massage from Camron when she got home.

"Hey," she greeted him when she opened the front door. He was in the living room watching sports highlights.

"Hey, baby." They shared a brief kiss.

"Where's TJ?"

"He's taking a nap. He was so wild earlier, I think he wore himself out."

Ce'Anna sighed with relief. "Thank God I wasn't here for that."

Camron smirked. "You'll get your turn tomorrow." Ce'Anna and Camron switched off duties every other day during the week so the other could have a much-needed break from Trent Junior. He was deeply loved, but a handful, as many young children were.

"Oh, before I hop in the shower, remember that girl I told you about from the gym? Camaiyah?"

Camron's eyebrows creased like he was trying to remember.

"Well, anyway, we exchanged numbers today, and we plan to hang out soon."

Camron smiled. "That's great! I'm glad you met a new friend."

"Right. Me too." Ce'Anna's heart panged with regret. She remembered all too well why she no longer associated with her old friends. Natasha and Rachel had stopped talking to her after she was exposed for sleeping with Xaveon, Natasha's boyfriend. Ce'Anna knew that Camron remembered this too, because she was also cheating on her ex-husband, Trent, with him, and he felt sorry for her, which touched her heart but annoyed her at the same time. Guilt nagged at her conscience when she thought of the implications of becoming friends with Camaiyah, particularly where it had to do with Camaiyah's sexy cousin, Jermaine.

She quickly made her way to the bathroom before Camron could see her guilty face.

***

The next day, Ce'Anna decided to head to the health store a few blocks away from the gym to get a multivitamin. She heard that those along with certain supplements helped to your muscles to heal more quickly after a strenuous workout like the ones she and Camaiyah were engaging in with the class at the gym.

She strode into the store, humming one of her jams from the radio that had just been playing in the car before she arrived.

She ran her finger across a few of the bottles of Black Seed oil. She hadn't come to this store for that in particular, but she had done some research and heard that it was good for you too.

"Hmmm," she breathed. "I wonder if the brands matter?"

"They shouldn't," said a catty voice behind her that she knew all too well. She slowly turned around to see Natasha and Rachel standing right behind her. Natasha was the one speaking. "Or maybe it's just a problem for you to see that specifically since you never could just stick to one thing."

Ce'Anna's face flushed. *They're really doing this in a health store?*

"Look, I didn't come here to fight. I haven't seen you guys since everything happened."

Natasha's eyes narrowed. "You mean since you slept with my boyfriend - the love of my life - behind my back?"

A lady standing nearby who was eavesdropping on their conversation gasped.

"That's right everybody!" Rachel joined in. "This bitch right here," she gestured toward Ce'Anna like she was a piece of trash, "This bitch right here can't be trusted. She's a slut."

"Excuse me. Do I need to call the police?" said the cashier. He looked like he was halfway enjoying Rachel and Natasha's little show, but didn't want to get in trouble at the same time if things really went left.

29

"No," said Ce'Anna. She put the bottle of Black Seed oil that she had taken off the shelf back in its place. "No need to call the police. I'll leave."

"Yeah bitch. Bounce," said Natasha.

"And learn how to stay your ass with one man," said Rachel. "Xaveon told Natasha you approached him recently. I would hate for Camron to find out about that, seeing as he is your new husband and all."

Ce'Anna was on her way out the door, but once she heard those words, she snapped.

"Listen, you ugly bitch!" she spat at Rachel. "Just because you couldn't find a man to save your fucking life, no matter how much we tried to hook you up with somebody, doesn't give you the right to keep coming at me. Instead of worrying so much about what I'm doing, you need to step your own game up and figure out why nobody wants you."

With those words, Ce'Anna darted out of the store as Rachel lunged in her direction.

Thankfully for her, Natasha and the cashier were holding her back.

# Chapter 4

The next day after Ce'Anna put TJ to sleep, she found herself thinking about Xaveon again. She had been thinking about him ever since that day he rejected her at the mall. She had no idea that she'd hurt him when she lied about not having a husband while they were sleeping together. And she also wondered why he neglected to tell her he was still in contact with Natasha? Not like it was her business anyway, but... Her thoughts were distracted when she heard TJ stir on his sleeping mat. She glanced over at him as he changed positions and continued his nap.

Ce'Anna opened her laptop and decided to check out Xaveon's social media page to see if he had posted anything new lately.

She saw a few new photos, but no signs of any women in his life.

She stared at the message button as if she had heard it calling her name. She wanted to reach out to him so badly. She knew she couldn't call him because he had blocked her number when he found out about Trent.

She took a deep breath then decided to shoot him a quick message.

*Hey.*

She stared at the message window. A few seconds later, there was a notification that he had seen it. Then, three dots appeared at the bottom of the screen, and her heart beat fast as she waited for his message to appear. This would either be really good or really bad.

*What do you want?*

She paused. *Should I even be writing him?* Camron's face flashed across her mind, and even Trent's, but she couldn't help herself.

*I just want to talk. Despite what happened, we can still be friends.*

*I thought we already went through this at the mall. Don't you already have a new husband? Tell that nigga to fill your needs.*

Though Xaveon was clearly rejecting her, Ce'Anna felt herself growing desperate. She missed him. His touch, his aggressive edge, his hands all over her body... She snapped out of it and sent him another message.

*Can I just come over so we can talk about this in person?*

Ce'Anna stared at the screen, waiting for his response. At first, it looked like he wasn't going to write back, but then the three dots appeared again.

*Look, I already told you my position in this situation, but you don't seem to know how to take no for an answer. I already told you I don't do married chicks. Stick with your husband. I ain't got shit for you over here.*

She felt like she almost had him. Why else would he still be responding?

*Why can't we just talk?*

"Come on, Xae!" she whined in frustration.

Then her frustration quickly dissipated when her eyes scanned his next response.

*Bitch, can't you read? I already told you I had no words. If you want to come over, you can top me off, but that's about it. Other than that, I got nothing for you.*

Ce'Anna stared at the screen in disgust. *This is how he feels, after our whole situation?* She knew she was wrong, but he didn't have to be rude. She closed the message app in frustration, blowing out a deep breath. Then she went back in to block Xaveon's profile before shutting down her laptop.

"Guess we're done for good."

After her failed conversation with Xaveon, Ce'Anna couldn't think of anything else to do with herself, so she turned on the TV. TJ had woken and up and was quietly playing with his toys, a welcome change from his usual demands of, "Play with me, Mommy!"

She flipped through the channels then stopped at a talk show where a woman's emphatic hand gestures caught her eye.

"I'm telling you, both men and women really need to hear this!" She looked at the show host then glanced at the audience. "If you can't learn to be content with your own life—who you are, what you have—you will never be happy. That's the bottom line. We need to stop being greedy and learn to be grateful!"

Ce'Anna quickly changed the channel before she could hear another word. Nothing else good seemed to be on, so she gave up and turned off the TV. She decided to play with her son until Camron came home.

Later that night, when she was wide awake at two in the morning, she couldn't get that woman's words out of her head.

Ce'Anna decided to go to the gym early the next morning to blow off some steam. She was still upset about Xaveon's refusal to talk to her. She only had about thirty minutes before she had to get back home to get TJ ready for daycare, but she figured that was enough time to work up a sweat.

When she entered the gym, she noticed it was mostly empty. "I guess most people don't wake up this early," she murmured, and made her way to the treadmills. Her heart rate increased when she saw Jermaine Cooper using one of the treadmills. It suddenly occurred to her that this was probably the only time he had to work out before the day got busy, and she filed that away in her memory as useful information.

She set up shop at the machine next to his. "Hey," she said with a smile.

He appeared to be deep in thought. After a beat, he finally noticed her.

"I'm sorry. Did you say something?"

"I was just saying hi. I'm Ce'Anna. We met a few weeks ago...you might remember...."

He paused then smiled in recollection. "Yeah, you're friends with my cousin Camaiyah, right?"

"Yup!" She turned on her machine to match his stride, and secretly worried that it was a quicker pace than she was used to. *I hope I'm not sweating and puffing within five minutes at this brisk pace,* she mused.

"So how do you like the gym so far? I know you and Camaiyah are taking the cardio class."

"It's great!" She took a deep breath to hide the fact that she was actually panting a bit already. "I really like the class."

He looked pleased with her response, so she decided to venture a little further to see if he would take the bait.

"I mean, it's not the type of workout I usually prefer to get my heart pumping, but I guess it will do for now." She shot him a coy glance to ensure he got the message.

He blushed. He wasn't sure what to say in response, so he let it slide.

She sensed his discomfort and backed off a little. "So, have you always wanted to own a gym?"

"Not really. I've always been into fitness, but the idea for the gym kind of came to me one day while I was talking with my boys Vel and Drew about how we needed to expand our personal trainer business. They agreed, and we all went in together for this place."

Ce'Anna stared at him in admiration.

36

"What?" He blushed again.

"That is so sexy, when a man knows what he wants."

Jermaine opened his mouth to respond, but Ce'Anna's alarm went off on her cell phone.

"Oh, shoot!" She quickly turned off her treadmill. "I need to... I've gotta get to an appointment!"

Jermaine turned his treadmill off as well. "Well, I'm about finished with my warm-up. It's about to get busy in here, the people who show up before work. Always does about this time. Catch you later."

Ce'Anna was already on her way out the door. "See you!" She yelled over her shoulder, then dashed out to her car.

Camron and TJ were probably both awake by this time, and she hadn't told Camron she was stepping out.

"I hope he doesn't start questioning me," she muttered, as she started up her car and headed home, turning up the radio to block out her conscience.

*** 

Camaiyah had a good day at work. She breezed through all of her clients, and everyone left her a hefty tip. If there wasn't anything else she was good with, she was good with her hands. She hummed as she made her way to her car, ready to go to the liquor store to end her day just right.

On her way to the store, she got a call. When she saw the caller ID, she was instantly annoyed.

"Ce'Anna?" She wrinkled her nose. "Ugh, I hope she doesn't kill my vibe."

She answered the call before the ring ran out.

"Hello?"

"Hey, Camaiyah. How are you?"

Camaiyah readjusted herself in her seat before she answered. "I'm good. And you?"

Ce'Anna let out a deep breath. "I need to talk to someone."

Camaiyah almost blurted, *Bitch, who said I was a therapist?* but then she remembered that she and Ce'Anna were supposed to be starting a friendship.

"Oh wow, what's going on?" She hoped she sounded more concerned than she felt.

"I really just need to get some things off my chest."

"About...?"

"I would rather talk in person."

Camaiyah rolled her eyes and let Ce'Anna prattle on.

"How about we stop for coffee after the next cardio class? You're going, right?"

Camaiyah mustered up a chipper response. "Yup!" *I am most definitely going.* Whatever Ce'Anna had to tell her must be big, and Camaiyah was kind of proud of herself for sticking with the cardio class. She had actually lost a few pounds. It hadn't done much to reduce her size yet, but at least it was a start, and she had to admit she felt more energetic lately.

"Okay, see you then," said Ce'Anna, but Camaiyah barely heard her because she was already ending the call and setting her phone in the cupholder.

She pulled into the parking lot of the liquor store and found a space. When she turned off the engine and looked at the entrance, she froze. Kay'Ceon was standing outside the store smoking a cigarette.

She sucked her teeth. "I really do not want to deal with him today."

She got out of her car after debating whether she should even be drinking tonight, and casually made her way to the entrance like she didn't see him.

Kay'Ceon's eyes lit up when he saw her. "Camaiyah!" His eyes traveled up and down her body.

She crossed her arms over her chest. *I don't know why I ever messed with his janky ass in the first place.* "What are you doing in my neighborhood?" she demanded.

"I was about to go in to get some drinks. You want to chill tonight?"

"I already told you I was done with that chapter of my life."

"I'm saying, though, we ain't gotta be in a relationship or nothing. We could just fulfill each other's needs, if you know what I mean, and I know you got needs, girl."

His eyes made her feel dirty, and his words stung. From what June told her a few months ago, Kay'Ceon had begged her for an actual relationship before she cut him off, but with Camaiyah, he only wanted her for sex.

This just made her blood boil, and not in a good way. She didn't need his mess right now. "Bye, Kay'Ceon." She pushed past him to go into the store.

"Camaiyah!"

She flipped him off and kept walking.

Once she got inside, she was happy to see there were no toothless old men trying to holla.

She grabbed her bottle of Henny and made her way to the cashier. *He is sexy as hell.* She took in his features and remembered how he'd kicked Mr. Toothless out that day, defending her honor. *Yes, bae, come to Mama. You're the kind*

40

*of man I need.* He was tall, caramel skinned, and had sexy, rugged features.

She placed her bottle in front of him on the counter.

He rang it up wordlessly, then he spoke. "Do you drink every night?"

*Damn, can I catch a break today?* It seemed like ever since she left work, people were on her back. Ce'Anna wanted to have a heart to heart. Kay'Ceon wanted her for sex. And now the cashier was trying to down her for drinking, and he bashed her fleeting fantasy of snagging his attention in a good way.

She challenged him with her eyes. "What's wrong with having a little something to relax?"

"That's a lot of relaxing. Ain't this your third bottle this week?"

Her face flushed, but she tried not to show it. "And? Why you sweating me? You keep track of all your customers like that?"

"You know, too much alcohol is not good for your body." He put it in a paper bag and handed it to her.

She snatched it. "Don't you work at a fucking liquor store?" She gestured around her for emphasis.

He held up his hands in surrender. "Look, I'm just trying to look out for you."

"Yeah?" Her eyes narrowed. "And why would you want to do that? I don't hear you giving sermons to any other customer you ring up." She was tired of the games these men played. It seemed like any time anyone she was halfway interested in seemed interested in her, it was only for sex. She was done. She may not be one of these skinny chicks that they all seemed to fall all over themselves for, but she still had dignity.

"Look, I'm not trying to start trouble with you. If you don't want my advice, you don't have to take it."

His tone was rough, but it was sexy-rough, and it suddenly pierced her offended pride that he cared. He was actually being sincere.

*And now I've ruined it!*

"Thank you for your concern," she said all prim and proper, not sure how else to wriggle out of this awkward encounter. She straightened her back, held her head high, and walked out of the store like a queen departing an audience with one of her courtiers. Luckily, Kay'Ceon was no longer loitering about.

As she got in her car and started the engine, the cashier's words echoed in her mind. Part of her wanted to believe that he was genuine and that he might even be interested in her, but her insecurities took over.

*Bitch, please. He's probably no different from all the other men who want to use you then dump you for someone better.*

\*\*\*

Try as she might, even a full bottle of Henny later, Camaiyah could not get the cashier's words out of her head.

Usually the Henny would get her right, but she felt so bad about the way she handled the situation that it continued to eat away at her despite her efforts to drown it all away with alcohol.

She stared at the empty bottle on the table in front of her until her eyes blurred.

Then she heard a knock at her door.

"Who is that?" she said to no one, because no one was there with her.

*You're a fucking alcoholic,* her mind told her. *You just sit here every day, alone and miserable because nobody wants to be around you and nobody wants to be with you either.*

The knock on the door sounded again, breaking her out of her thoughts.

She made her way to the door, halfway hoping it was Coop with another bottle.

But then she remembered - he was probably with that bitch June - and she had made him stop drinking anyway.

"Bougie little bitch is turning my cousin into a fucking lame," she breathed, then she flung the door open without even asking who was knocking.

There stood Kay'Ceon.

"What are you doing here?" Camaiyah narrowed her eyes at him.

"I'm saying though... We never got to finish our conversation at the liquor store." He held up a bottle of Henny. "I brought your favorite."

Camaiyah eyed the bottle. She suddenly felt thirsty, but she knew Kay'Ceon could not be trusted.

"And what makes you think I want to drink with you?"

Kay'Ceon took a step forward. "Come on, Camaiyah. I know you miss this."

His voice was so husky, it almost intoxicated her more than the Henny did.

But she couldn't give in to him again, just so he could play her like he did last time.

"That's where you're wrong. I don't miss you. I want nothing to do with you. Go away."

"Camaiyah. Stop trying to play me. You said it yourself that you felt like you loved me."

She paused. *I can't believe he just went there.*

Kay'Ceon had broken her heart in the worst way, but she wasn't about to stand here and take what was left of her dignity today.

"Get the fuck away from my apartment, Kay'Ceon. And don't come back."

When Kay'Ceon finally realized that he wasn't getting any, he showed his true colors as Camaiyah knew he would.

"Fine," he sucked his teeth. "I was just trying to do you a favor anyway."

"Do me a favor? Fuck you mean, do me a favor?"

"Nobody wants no fat ass bitch like you. That's why you ain't never been with another nigga since me, and probably had nobody before me."

Camaiyah's breath almost caught in her throat.

In one swift motion, she roughly pushed Kay'Ceon out of her doorway.

He was caught off guard, so he almost fell.

Camaiyah slammed her door in his face and locked it before sinking to the floor.

"Yeah, that's right. You a fat ass bitch!" Kay'Ceon said through the door, then a few moments later, she heard his car door slam before he peeled off.

Camaiyah sat on the floor hugging herself for a long time, until she could no longer take it.

"I need another fucking bottle," she said, then grabbed her keys to go to the liquor store.

*\*\*\**

As promised, Ce'Anna was at the cardio class bright and early.

Camaiyah walked in and tried to look friendly, but honestly, she wanted nothing more than to go back home and stay in bed. She still had a serious headache from the night before. After she had downed that first bottle of Henny, then had the argument with Kay'Ceon, she had driven drunk to a different liquor store to pick up another one.

*I really got to slow down.*

Ce'Anna didn't seem to notice that Camaiyah's expression said *Don't speak to me.* "So, you ready for this class?" she said in her usual chipper voice.

"Mm hm." Camaiyah took a sip from her water bottle for something distracting to do. She stood still and gazed at the floor as she fought down a wave of nausea.

Other students started to make their way into the room.

Ce'Anna pressed on. "Listen, I know we were supposed to have coffee today after class, but I forgot I had to bring my son to a doctor's appointment."

*Son?* Camaiyah's head snapped toward Ce'Anna. "Oh, okay, that's fine."

"Sorry." Ce'Anna shot her a weak smile. "Can we reschedule for another day?"

"Yup."

The teacher walked in and the class began.

Throughout the workout, aside from trying to make her head stop swimming, Camaiyah kept sneaking glances at Ce'Anna's body. She saw no sign of the usual belly bulge left over from being pregnant, even after one kid. *She's probably never had to struggle with weight, and her perfect body snapped right back as soon as she pushed him out.* She rolled her eyes at the thought.

To her credit, Camaiyah was able to keep up with the class more than Ce'Anna was, even being hungover. She might be out of shape, but she was blessed with a naturally strong build. *At least I got something on her.*

Once the class was over, Ce'Anna had to rush out, and Camaiyah was grateful because she didn't feel like faking friendliness any longer.

***

Later on that night, Camaiyah got a text from her aunt Karyn.

*Haven't seen you in a while. Have you thought about what we discussed?*

Camaiyah stared at the message until her eyes blurred, then she put her phone on her nightstand and went to sleep.

# Chapter 5

Camaiyah was sitting in her living room enjoying a drink by herself. The day had gone smoothly thus far, but she kept getting the feeling that her peace would be short lived.

Almost as soon as the thought crossed her mind, she heard a knock on her front door. She rolled her eyes as she put her drink down to go answer it.

"Who is it?"

"It's me!" Coop called from the other side.

She opened the door and watched Coop as he walked past her into the apartment. He sat down on her couch, fuming.

"What's wrong with you? You want a drink?"

"No, I'm still trying to cut back. June doesn't like me drinking like that."

Camaiyah sucked her teeth as she made her way to sit next to him.

"You seem to be dead set on letting that girl run your damn life."

"Look, Camaiyah. You and June gonna have to come to some kind of agreement. This whole beef between you two is stressing me."

"Where is this coming from?"

"Don't try to act like you don't know. It seems like every time me and June get together, she complains about you, and every time I see you, you taking shots at her."

"Well, I wouldn't need to take shots if she would learn to keep her mouth shut!"

"Enough!" Cooped exclaimed so loud that he startled Camaiyah, and she leaned back in surprise when he jumped to his feet.

"I'm going to need you to simmer down," she said, holding her hand over her heart.

"No, I'm-a need you to simmer down. June is my girl. You need to get over it, or I'm-a—"

"You'll do what, Coop?" Camaiyah rolled her neck as she set her drink on the table and shot him a pointed glance. "Or what?" She crossed her arms over her chest and waited.

Coop sighed. This conversation was going nowhere.

"Look, Camaiyah, you been my favorite cousin for as long as I can remember. If anybody would be happy for me, I would think it would be you. But all you seem to do now is bring drama into my life and in my relationship with June, like you're trying to drive a wedge between us."

"Oh, so now you trying to blame all your problems on me?"

"Camaiyah, do you even realize that if you and June had fought at the gym that day, you could have cost me a lot of business?"

"Did you go as hard with her as you're going with me?"

"Shit, Camaiyah! Can you even hear me? Look outside yourself for once. I'm in love with her!"

Coop's words hit her like a slap in the face. *In love? What the hell does he mean, in love?* She tried to collect herself.

"I can't believe you are even putting her on the same level as me. We are family. You've only known her for months."

"Well, if we family, you need to act like it." He got up to leave.

"Where are you going?"

"I can't talk to you right now, Camaiyah. You not even hearing me."

He opened the front door. "Love you."

"Love you too."

He closed the door behind him.

***

Ce'Anna and Camron had taken separate cars to work because Ce'Anna had a parent-teacher conference, and Camron had to pick up TJ.

When Ce'Anna walked in the house, Camron was sitting in the kitchen with the lights off, a bottle of Heinekin on the table in front of him. He took a sip when he saw her but said nothing.

Ce'Anna's heart dropped. "What happened? Why are you sitting here drinking in the dark? Where's TJ?" Her head started pounding. *Lord, please. Not my baby.*

"He's upstairs... sleep." Camron's tone was dry, and his words were slow.

Ce'Anna's anxiety subsided. "Okay, then what's up?"

He sighed and sat back. "Why don't you tell me, Ce'Anna?"

She stared blankly. "I'm not following."

"Oh yeah?" His voice slurred slightly. He pulled out his phone and unlocked it. "Let's see the messages I got from Xaveon today."

The color drained from Ce'Anna's face as Camron opened his message app and read the first one out loud. "You need to learn how to keep your bitch on a leash."

"Camron, I can explain—"

"Of course, being the clueless idiot you've turned me into, I respond that I have no idea what he's talking about."

"Camron—"

"But wait! It gets better! He actually sent me some screenshots."

Ce'Anna stood there feeling sick to her stomach as Camron read the messages between her and Xaveon the day he rejected her and she blocked him for good.

When he was finished, Camron stared at her, his expression unreadable. "So you want to explain this to me?"

"Camron, I'm sorry." A tear rolled down her cheek.

"Did you fuck him?" His words shot out as if they were expelled from a shotgun.

"What?"

He stood up and walked over to where Ce'Anna stood frozen in place. He got right in her face and said, "Did you go over his house that night, and did you fuck him?"

"Of course not!"

"Of course not? Why the hell would I be surprised if you did? It's not like you weren't fucking him while we were together before we got married!"

Camron was standing so close that flecks of spit landed on her face as he spoke. She could smell the alcohol on his breath.

"Look, we need to talk about this later." She wiped her face. "Right now, you're drunk."

Camron grabbed his coat. "I can't stay in this house with you."

"Where are you going?"

"My parents' house. They already know I'm coming."

"How are you going to get there? You're drunk!"

"I am capable of thinking for myself, Ce'Anna. I ordered a Lyft. It's already outside."

He walked past her and grabbed a suitcase from the floor near the front door. Ce'Anna hadn't noticed it.

"How long are you staying?"

"Who knows, Ce'Anna? If you didn't want me, you shouldn't have married me." His voice broke.

*I hurt him.* Her heart gripped her throat. "Camron, don't say that!"

She watched him open the door and stumble down the front steps to the waiting car.

"Camron!" she yelled, but it was no use. They were already driving off.

She slowly made her way back into her house as the gravity of the situation finally sank in.

She was losing everything – again.

***

Camaiyah was stewing after her argument with Coop. *I can't believe he is trying to take that bitch's side over mine.* She could admit that she was wrong for catfishing June, but that didn't give June any right to try to break up Camaiyah's friendship with Coop. I mean, he was *her* cousin!

Camaiyah jumped when her cell phone rang.

"Hello?"

"Camaiyah..." She could hear Ce'Anna crying through the phone.

"Girl, what's wrong with you?"

"I really need to talk right now. Are you home? Can I come over?"

"Um...okay. Yeah. Are you bringing your son?"

"No, I'm going to drop him off at my mom's house. I think I need a drink."

Damn, she must really be going through it. "Oh okay. Come on then."

"What's your address?"

"I'll text it to you."

After they hung up, Camaiyah texted Ce'Anna her address then threw on her coat to head to the liquor store for more bottles. She didn't know Ce'Anna's preferences, so she decided she would get an assortment.

She knew she shouldn't be driving with the slight buzz she already had going, but she had driven under the influence multiple times before. "I hope my ass don't get into another accident." She already had two DUIs, and one more meant she would lose her license.

She made it to the liquor store in one piece. She quickly found bottles of Bacardi, Grey Goose, Absolut, and Smirnoff, along with her usual bottle of Henny.

The cashier's eyes widened as she placed the bottles before him.

"Damn, girl! You want to talk about it?"

"It's not for me, asshole. It's for a friend."

He picked up one of the bottles as if he was inspecting it. "You know, alcohol ain't the only way to solve problems."

"Who are you, Dr. Phil? Just ring me up please."

He stared at her more intently. "Have you been drinking today already?"

"Look, why are you asking me all these questions?"

"Your demeanor is off. I can tell you a little tipsy."

"Okay, are you a cop and this job is your side hustle or something? Are you going to arrest me, or what? Because I have to get back home."

"You know you shouldn't be driving like that."

Camaiyah almost had to squeeze her legs together to keep from lunging across the counter at him like a wildcat in heat. The sexiness of his husky voice was almost too much for her. "My two DUIs already told me that. Can you ring me up, or are these on the house?"

He stared at her for a second longer then reluctantly rang up her bottles.

She drummed her nails on the counter as he double bagged them with paper and plastic for her, taking more time than he needed to.

"Thank you," she said in a singsong voice then turned toward the door.

"Wait."

She turned back. His face was full of concern.

"Shit," he muttered under his breath. He grabbed a used scratch-off lottery ticket and scribbled something on the back of it. "Here." He handed it to her.

She stared at him as she took it. "What's this?" Her eyes shifted to his writing.

"My name is Rashad. Just call me as soon as you get home, okay? Please."

Camaiyah almost dropped the bag of bottles. She stared back and forth between him and his name and number. She wasn't sure how to take this. "Why?"

"Just do it. Okay?"

"Fine." She turned and made her way out to her car.

When she got home, she sat in her car for a few moments trying to process what had just happened. *Why was he so concerned?* She had never before experienced that with a man. Usually, it was all about sex, but Rashad had made it clear that he cared about her.

"But he doesn't even know me!" she exclaimed. Camaiyah was confused. Her eyes blurred as they filled with tears. She quickly blinked them back when she realized that she had pulled into a parking space directly behind Ce'Anna's car in her apartment parking lot. Suddenly she remembered why she'd returned to the liquor store in the first place.

"Damn, this bitch here already?"

She fired off a quick text to Rashad before going inside.

*Hey. It's Camaiyah. I'm home.*

He responded within seconds.

*Good. Stay out of trouble, and please don't drive anywhere else tonight.*

*I won't.*

She got out of her car as Ce'Anna exited hers.

It was clear that Ce'Anna had been crying.

"Thank you for letting me come over."

"No problem."

They walked up to Camaiyah's apartment and went inside.

Camaiyah flipped the light switch. "Make yourself at home. I'll get us some cups."

Ce'Anna sat on the couch as Camaiyah set the bag of bottles on the coffee table next to the half-empty bottle of Henny then made her way to the kitchen.

When she returned, Ce'Anna was just sitting there staring into space.

"I wasn't sure what you liked, so I got a variety." Camaiyah removed the bottles from the bag.

Ce'Anna shook her head. "Honestly, it doesn't even matter. I'm not much of a drinker, but I need to get plastered right now."

Camaiyah stared at her for a second. "Okay... So let's start you off with some Grey Goose." She poured about half a cup and handed it to Ce'Anna then poured herself some Henny.

Ce'Anna downed it before Camaiyah had a chance to settle herself on the sofa.

"Damn, girl! You might need to slow down." *Now I sound like Rashad's Dr. Phil ass.* She smiled at the thought of him.

Ce'Anna shook her head. "Oh, don't worry about me. I'm a big girl." She reached for the Grey Goose and poured herself some more.

*Well, alrighty then.* "So, what's going on?"

Ce'Anna took a sip, then nodded. "I think my husband is going to leave me."

*Husband? This bitch is just full of surprises.* "I didn't know you were married."

"Yeah, I'm sorry. I didn't tell you."

"Well, it's not like it was any of my business or anything."

"I know, but I was kind of flirting with your cousin—"

"Flirting with my cousin! When?" Camaiyah sat up, ready to hear this tea.

Ce'Anna's face reddened. "Oh, I thought he might have told you."

"No, he didn't. What happened?"

Camaiyah listened with great intrigue as Ce'Anna spilled the beans. The more she talked, the more she poured Grey Goose, and the drunker she got. She got a little loose as the story wore on, first talking about her crush on Coop, then on her fight with her husband, then her divorce from her previous husband.

Camaiyah felt like she had heard the girl's whole life story by the time she finished. *Damn, she a THOT THOT.*

"So, what do you think I should do?"

By now, Ce'Anna was lit. Most of that bottle of Grey Goose was gone.

Camaiyah opened her mouth to respond, but in that exact moment, she heard a knock on her door.

"Who is that?" Camaiyah asked, as if Ce'Anna knew.

Ce'Anna giggled. "Girl, I don't know! Go answer!" She gestured with both arms and almost fell off the couch.

Camaiyah snickered. "Bitch, you lit." She was feeling kind of nice herself, but she was nowhere near as drunk as Ce'Anna.

Camaiyah strode to her front door but tripped on the corner of her carpet before she made it.

Both she and Ce'Anna burst out laughing.

"Ooh, watch your step!" Ce'Anna howled, holding her belly.

"Shit, I'm 'bout to pee!" Tears streamed down Camaiyah's face as she laughed at herself.

The knocking was more emphatic this time.

"Okay, okay, I'm coming." Camaiyah composed herself to open the door.

There stood Coop.

"Cousin, what you doing here?" she demanded.

"Hey," he said, and he smiled as he leaned in and tried to look past her. "What's all this craziness going on in here? You realize how loud you are, right?"

Camaiyah cocked her head at him. "Are you high?" From the redness of his eyes and the smell that was emanating from his clothes, she already had her answer.

"I just needed to relax." He held up a bottle of Patron. "You wanna drink on something?"

She opened the door to let him in. "Boy, I already started." She eyed his drink. "And from the looks of that bottle, so did you!"

He smiled and followed her to the living room. He saw Ce'Anna and stopped in his tracks. "Hey! I didn't know you were here..."

"Hey!" She waved at him enthusiastically. "Come join all this craziness!"

His eyes widened at the bottles on Camaiyah's table. "Damn, y'all is twisted!" He slurred his words.

"No, baby. *You* is twisted." She directed him to the couch next to Ce'Anna.

She returned to her own seat and watched as they eyed each other, then a thought occurred to her. "Wait, your precious June ain't mad that you drinking and smoking weed?"

Coop's smile dropped as he shrugged his shoulders. "She broke up with me."

*"What?"*

He took a sip from his bottle of Patron.

"Yup. She said I had to choose between her or you, so I told her that wasn't fair. She can't make me drop my family."

"I know that's right," Camaiyah said, though she felt kind of guilty that she had a hand in their breakup.

"Well, it looks like ain't none of us gonna be in a relationship by the end of tonight!" Ce'Anna sang. She looked at Camaiyah. "Girl, why don't you put on some music?"

"Sure!" Camaiyah tuned her stereo system to the radio, and her favorite station was playing all the party songs.

Ce'Anna immediately got up and started dancing, almost causing Camaiyah to spit out her drink at her lack of rhythm.

Coop was much less discreet. He did spit out his drink when he burst out laughing. "Ah, shit! Ah, shit!" He slapped his knee as he rocked with laughter. "You can't dance for shit!"

Ce'Anna was unfazed. "Oh really? Let's see you do better." She gestured for Coop to join her.

"Bet," Coop replied. He set down his bottle, wiped his mouth with the back of his hand, and joined Ce'Anna.

It was a comical sight, and Camaiyah was tempted to take a video of them, but she couldn't do her cousin like that, though it would definitely fuck with June, and that would be fun...

She watched as Coop and Ce'Anna got cozy. She even got up and tried to show Ce'Anna how to twerk properly. CeAnna didn't get it.

After a little while, the station started playing slow songs, and Ce'Anna and Coop slow-danced together.

Their moves became much more sensual, and Camaiyah had half a mind to tell them to stop. But another side of her felt like this would be the final nail in the coffin for Coop and June's relationship.

She had a smug little thought. *She would never forgive him if he slept with another girl.*

Camaiyah excused herself to go to the bathroom, but it was really so Coop and Ce'Anna could be alone together.

She heard their muffled voices through the door as she eavesdropped. *I'm so bad,* she thought, but she couldn't help it. There was some serious flirting going on, along with some heavy petting judging from Ce'Anna's soft moans.

She heard them collapse onto the couch, and she knew the fire had started.

Her conscience kept pleading with her to stop them, but she simply didn't want to.

*I'm in love with her!*

Coop's words came back to her, and she knew that she had to make a decision: To do right by her cousin, or to fulfill her own selfish desires.

"Shit!" she huffed. She banged open the bathroom door to hopefully startle them before she made an appearance in the living room. Yep, sure enough, she had caught them just before things got down and dirty. Ce'Anna was stripped down to her bra and panties, and was straddling Coop's lap.

"Okay, okay, that's enough," Camaiyah announced. She coaxed Ce'Anna off of her cousin.

"What are you doing?" said Coop.

"Y'all are both drunk. Ce'Anna, put your clothes back on, please."

"We were just having fun!" Ce'Anna pouted.

"You don't need to have that kind of fun tonight." She sucked her teeth and handed Ce'Anna her clothes. "Come on, girl, put your clothes on."

Ce'Anna stumbled into her jeans then pulled her top over her head, struggling with the armholes because she was so wasted. "Damn it!" she exclaimed, and finally got it on straight.

Camaiyah looked back and forth between the two of them. "Ce'Anna, I'm going to let you sleep in my spare bedroom. Coop, you got the couch."

"I don't want to go to bed!" Ce'Anna whined.

Camaiyah almost burst out laughing at her little tantrum, but she knew the girl wasn't in her right mind.

"Come on." She gently guided her to the bedroom, making sure she propped up enough pillows for her to sleep upright. She stayed with her for another half hour to keep her calm and make sure she stayed in bed.

After that, she went out to check on Coop, but he was already asleep on the couch.

She returned to the guest bedroom and sat with Ce'Anna until she fell asleep.

Camaiyah was so tired and desperate for sleep herself, but she didn't want to leave either of them alone, so she set her alarm to wake up every hour to check on them.

Coop woke up first the next morning. Camaiyah was already in the kitchen making breakfast and coffee.

"Hey, cuz," he mumbled.

"Hey."

"I fucked up last night."

"You remember everything that happened?"

He nodded.

"How are you feeling?"

"I'll be fine, but I gotta talk to June."

"You're going to tell her?"

"I can't just leave it like that."

"Well, if that's what you think is best. You want something to eat?"

"No, thanks. I'd better get going." He readied himself to go. "I'll catch you later."

"See you."

Ce'Anna slept for another hour after Coop left. When she woke, she didn't remember where she was, much less what she had done the night before. She sat there in shock as Camaiyah filled her in on the details.

"Oh my gosh, I am never drinking again!"

"Girl, it's fine. Nothing happened. You were having a rough night."

"Yeah, but I still kissed him and tried to have sex with him. If I tell Camron about this, he may never take me back."

"Well, I can't help you with that part, but if you really want to be with him, the best you can do is try."

"Thank you. And thank you for stopping us before things went too far."

Camaiyah nodded and forced a smile. "Yeah, sure. No problem."

\*\*\*

When Camaiyah was finally alone, she was exhausted in more ways than one. She took a long nap to catch up on the sleep she missed the night before. When she woke up, she felt refreshed, but she didn't want to stay in the house all day, so she decided to go outside to get some air.

*I should have worn my big coat,* she mused as she shivered her way home after walking around the block.

When she got to her front steps, she heard tires squeal as a car swerved into the parking lot. Her nerves were so frazzled that she whipped her head around in a reflex action to see which direction it was coming from and jump out the way if she had to.

Her jaw dropped when she saw that it was June's car.

June threw the car in park and hopped out, ready for action.

*No, this bitch don't think she pulling up on me!* Camaiyah was in defense mode already.

June stalked toward her looking fierce and ready to fight. "You just don't know how to mind your damn business, do you?"

Camaiyah wasn't threatened by her stance. "Um, I think you need to simmer down and remember who you are talking to."

"Bitch, I'm talking to you!" She jabbed her manicured nail in Camaiyah's face. "I'm sick of you doing stupid shit to try to sabotage me and Jermaine's relationship."

"First of all, get your finger outta my face. Second, if y'all was such a good couple, what I do shouldn't matter."

"I'm fucking sick of you!" June lunged at Camaiyah and actually caught her off guard.

*Oh, so she trippin, trippin.*

June got one hit in before Camaiyah quickly gained advantage, easily blocking her blows and landing a few of her own. When she got sick of June's constant swinging, she grabbed her up in a bear hug and slammed her to the ground.

Camaiyah got on top of June, pinning her down with her weight as she pummeled her face and body.

"Get the hell off of my sister!"

Camaiyah heard Iliana's voice before she felt herself being yanked backward onto the ground by her hair. Before she could take a breath, Iliana was raining blows down on her face.

"Bitch! Bitch! Bitch!" She screamed in between each hit.

Camaiyah was soon defenseless as June and Iliana kicked and stomped her. She tried to grab at their legs to stop them, but they were moving too quickly.

Finally, one of her neighbors and his two sons broke them up, each grabbing one of them.

"So y'all just gonna jump me, passy ass bitches?" Camaiyah screamed, her nose bloody and her hair all over the place.

June's face looked lumped up too.

Iliana's face was red, but that was about it.

June turned to Iliana. "I told you not to come! I can handle this bitch myself!"

Camaiyah answered that retort. "Yeah, right, bitch! You wasn't handling shit! Your fucking baby sister had to save your life." She saw blood fly out of her mouth as she spoke, and that was enough to make her lunge toward

June again, but her neighbor's son held her back.

"Bitch, you need to stay out my fucking relationship!" June screamed. "You ain't nothing but a snake ass hating ass bitch!"

"Bitch, if it wasn't for me, you wouldn't even have a fucking relationship. I should have let him fuck her!"

June lunged toward Camaiyah, but Camaiyah's neighbor firmly held her in place.

"Look, ladies," said the neighbor's son who was holding Iliana back. "I don't know what's going on with all of you, but we are not going to stand here all day holding you back from each other. You all need to calm down, or we're calling the police."

Iliana visibly wilted. "Come on, June. She's not even worth it."

June stared at her sister, steam practically coming out of her ears. "Fine. Let's go."

Camaiyah's neighbor and his son escorted Iliana and June to their vehicles to ensure that another fight didn't break out. They stood on the side of the road watching until both their cars were down the street and out of sight.

"Okay, can you let me go now?" said Camaiyah. Her arms were hurting from being held behind her back. Her neighbor's other son released her.

"You know, you really shouldn't be out here fighting." He stared at her face. "Do you need an ambulance?"

"No, I don't need no fucking ambulance!" She knew her tone was a little too aggressive, but she was humiliated. *I can't believe those little bitches jumped me.* She went back into her apartment to examine her face in the mirror. She had a black eye and a busted lip.

When she gazed at her reflection, tears filled her eyes. "Look at this shit!" she wailed.

Anger flared within her, and she had half a mind to pull up on June to finish the altercation, but she knew June was right. She was a snake.

# Chapter 6

Camaiyah hibernated at home for the next two days, refusing to answer any calls or texts from anyone, including Coop. When he came by her house early that morning begging her to open the door, she pretended not to hear him.

*My life is a mess.* "Ugh, I need a damn drink!"

She didn't feel like going anywhere, but her urge for alcohol overcame her resistance, and she forced herself to put on some clothes and go to the liquor store. She hoped Rashad wasn't working that day. Her face still wasn't healed from the black eye June and Iliana had given her, and she was in no mood to hear any of his "concern."

When she pulled up to the store, she sat outside contemplating whether she should go in or go back home. She glanced at the cars in the parking lot and wished she knew which one was Rashad's. "Well, I came all the way out here," she muttered, and with a heavy sigh, she got out of her car.

As soon as she walked into the store, Rashad's eyes were on her.

"Damn, girl!" he exclaimed. "Who beat your ass?"

Camaiyah held her hand up to stop him from talking. "Not today, okay?" Her eyes filled up as she made her way to the Henny bottles.

She trudged to the counter hoping Rashad wouldn't give her any lip.

"What's wrong?" His demeanor had shifted when he noticed she wasn't in the mood.

Camaiyah opened her mouth to answer, but at that moment, two skinny girls walked into the store giggling and loudly talking. Camaiyah watched Rashad from the corner of her eye to see if he checked them out.

"Oh, this is a liquor store!" said one of the girls.

"I told you they didn't sell Pampers, bitch!" said the other girl, and they howled with laughter as they walked back outside.

"Dizzy broads," Camaiyah muttered under her breath. "Those girls are probably the type you go for, huh?" She smirked and slid her eyes at Rashad.

Rashad's eyebrow raised. "Negative. I like my women full figured." He licked his lips, and Camaiyah blushed at his admiration.

"Well, that's good to know," she said, and gave him a flirty smile. She didn't realize how comical she looked trying to be sexy with a puffy black eye, but Rashad was such a gentleman that he would never make a comment like that.

"I won't bother you today about this Henny," he said as he rang her up and put her bottle in a small paper bag. "But I do got a bone to pick with you about something else."

Camaiyah took the bag from him. "What could you possibly have a bone to pick with me about?"

"I see you haven't called me or texted me again since that night."

Camaiyah caught herself before her jaw dropped. *He likes me?*

"Called or texted you? I didn't get any notifications from you either."

Rashad shot her a cocky grin. "Well, it looks like we gonna have to fix that then, huh?"

"How we gonna fix it?" She stared into his eyes, her heart pounding with nervous anticipation.

Just then, a group of college kids walked into the store.

"I'll call you tonight," Rashad said.

"Okay!" Camaiyah nodded then turned to leave as another customer walked into the store.

As soon as she got in her car, a text pinged her phone. She quickly swiped her screen to check it, thinking it was Rashad, but it was her aunt Karyn.

*I know you are not at work today. I already called. You have been avoiding me since our last conversation, and I don't like it. I want you at my house within the hour.*

Camaiyah's face reddened as she took in the chastisement.

*Okay. I'm on my way.*

*Good.*

She drove the long route to her aunt's house to give herself time to think of what to tell her. She had been avoiding this conversation for a while, just like her aunt said, and she dreaded it.

When she pulled up, her aunt was standing at the front door behind the screen, waiting.

"Damn! Auntie wasn't playing," Camaiyah muttered. She got out of her car and trudged to the door with the words *walk of shame* blaring in her mind.

As soon as Camaiyah crossed the threshold, Aunt Karyn started in on her.

"Girl, look at your face!"

Camaiyah saw the look of disappointment in her eyes, so she kept her head down.

"Look at me," Aunt Karyn said, her tone kind but firm. She cupped Camaiyah's chin and gently lifted her face so they were eye to eye. "Camaiyah, you know you have to stop this. This is not the way."

A tear slid down Camaiyah's cheek. "I know," she sniffled.

"Come on, let's go sit in the living room."

Aunt Karyn led her to the couch and sat down next to her.

They sat there without a word while Camaiyah wiped her tears. Aunt Karyn finally spoke. "Listen, Camaiyah, what I am about to say might sound tough, but I am not saying it to hurt you. I love you like a daughter. You know that. But I can tell that something is eating you up inside. Something causes you to act out in the ways that you do. What is it, baby?"

"It's my weight." More tears flowed, and Camaiyah looked away.

"Your weight?" Aunt Karyn's voice was laced with concern. "What about your weight?" She handed Camaiyah a tissue.

"I've always been the fat girl." Camaiyah's voice croaked. "The one no one wants, but everyone has something to say about."

"Girl, you're not even that big! I mean, you could stand to lose a few pounds, but hell, so could I. Is that why you lash out at people, like your friend June?"

Camaiyah nodded, but she couldn't meet Karyn's eyes. She stared straight ahead with a faraway look in her eyes. "I felt like June always got what she wanted. I noticed it when we were younger, but I tried to ignore it, but then it became too much when she ended up getting with Kay'Ceon, a boy that I had been crushing on long before she even met him."

"She did this behind your back?" Aunt Karyn looked like she wanted to cuss June out if she did.

Camaiyah shook her head. "No. She didn't even know I liked him, but I did, so it still hurt. But he didn't even notice me. He went straight for her because she was skinny. At least that's what my mind told me."

"Did you ever reveal to her that you had feelings for him?"

"No. By that time, I had already turned against her in my mind, so I started flirting with him behind her back to see if I could get him to like me. I thought he did, but he ended up only wanting me for sex."

Camaiyah's ears were burning from the humiliation.

"Did you have sex with him?"

Camaiyah finally met her aunt's eyes, and Karyn could see the depth of shame in her niece's.

"Honey, we all make mistakes. You can say it if you did."

Camaiyah nodded. Her secret was finally out.

"Did you ever tell June this?"

"No. I felt at the time like she owed it to me. Plus her and Kay'Ceon kept breaking up and getting back together anyway."

"Have you been with any other guys since him? Ones that only wanted you for sex?"

"No. I kept to myself and turned all my rage against June. But even though I was doing her wrong, it still didn't take away the hurt, so I started drinking."

Camaiyah went on to explain that she had started drinking Henny a few times a week, but her drinking increased after the catfish situation blew up in her face.

Aunt Karyn just listened, her face devoid of judgment. When Camaiyah was finished, she took her time to speak.

"Do you feel like you might need counseling?"

Camaiyah shook her head. "I thought about it recently, but I think I'm going to just focus on my health instead. I've been taking a cardio class at Coop's gym, and it's been helping me feel better about myself. I've even lost a few pounds, though you might not be able to tell yet."

Aunt Karyn smiled. "I was going to say, you do look a bit thinner. That's great, Camaiyah. Cardio class is good." She paused. "What about the drinking?"

"Okay, full confession. I honestly just bought a bottle before you texted me. I didn't see it as a big issue until now, but I'm going to cut back."

"Do you think you might need help with that?"

"No. I want to try it myself first. If I can't, I'll seek help. The same with the counseling."

Aunt Karyn was quiet as she met Camaiyah's eyes. "Okay. I'm going to be checking in with you on both of those things to help keep you on track because I love you. I want you to be honest with me too. If either of these things seem like they become too much for you to handle alone, we need to get you into counseling, and possibly some other programs."

Camaiyah nodded. "Okay. That sounds fair."

***

After begging for what felt like the thousandth time, Camron finally agreed to meet with Ce'Anna. She took in his features as he walked through the door to their house.

"Where's TJ?" he asked as he removed his coat.

"He's at my mom's house." Ce'Anna took it and hung it up.

They made their way to the kitchen table and sat down across from each other. Camron noticed some papers on the table.

"What's that?" he nodded toward the papers.

"I'll explain later."

"That sounds ominous, but... okay."

Ce'Anna stared at him for several moments, willing herself not to cry. It seemed like that was all she'd been doing since he left. Camron's departure hurt her worse than Trent's because it felt like she'd made the same stupid mistake again. She had hurt another man who sincerely loved her, and she had no clue why, or how she could break this cycle.

"The first thing I want to say is that I'm sorry." Her bottom lip trembled, but she blinked back the tears that attempted to fall. *He needs to know I'm serious.*

Camron waited for her to continue.

"Camron, I know I messed up, really badly, especially since this already happened with us before, when I was with Xaveon, along with you and Trent."

Camron swallowed hard, and his eyes looked like he was choking back tears.

"I know that my actions lately have said otherwise, but I would never want to hurt you."

"Do you want to be married to me?" Camron blurted it like the question had been burning in his mind for years.

Ce'Anna was slightly taken aback. "Yes, I do."

"Are you sure?" Camron pressed. "Because I can't keep going in circles with you, Ce'Anna. I feel like I love you more than life itself, but a man can only take his woman cheating on him but so many times. I already stayed with you after the first time, and most wouldn't have done that."

Ce'Anna's cheeks reddened. "I know. I messed up. Well, we both did, because you knew I was married to Trent when we got together, but that's beside the point. I want to start over."

"How are we going to do that? How am I going to know that I'm the only man that has your attention, especially since this is the second time you've been involved with Xaveon?"

"I blocked him." She pulled out her phone to show him her block list, then she quickly tapped her social media account to show him that she had blocked him there too. "Even if he tries to contact me, which I doubt he will, he won't be able to. I'm done for good this time, I swear."

Camron's eyes begged her for the truth. "Did you sleep with him that night?"

"No."

"Ce'Anna...are you sure?"

"Yes, Camron. I actually blocked him from my social media that day."

He visibly relaxed his tense shoulders and sat back in his seat.

"But before we move forward, there is one other thing I have to tell you." Ce'Anna's heart pounded as she told him what happened with Jermaine at Camaiyah's house.

He sighed and shook his head. "Ce'Anna..."

"Wait. Please. Let me finish." She picked up the papers. "I cancelled my gym membership so I won't run into him again." She handed the first paper to him for proof. "And I signed up for counseling because..." She paused and sighed with resignation. "I think I might have a problem." She handed him the papers from her counselor's office.

He studied the documents then looked at her. "A problem?"

She nodded. "Yeah. I have to find out why I keep getting caught in these types of situations. I don't want to do anything like this ever again."

Camron stared at her like he didn't know what to think.

"I'm asking you for another chance, Camron. Please, honey. I know what I did was wrong, but I want to get it right. I don't want to lose what we have."

Camron opened his mouth to speak then shut it. He stood up and grabbed his coat.

Ce'Anna's heart sank. "You're leaving?"

He nodded. "I need time to think about this, Ce'Anna. This is a lot."

\*\*\*

After another week of seeing Camron at work, but not being able to talk to him because she wanted to give him some time, she was surprised one day to hear the front door open, and see Camron walk in holding a suitcase.

Her breath caught in her throat. "You're coming home?"

He gave her a small smile. "I'm coming home."

***

Camaiyah took the conversation she had with Aunt Karyn to heart. She continued the cardio classes at the gym, and had already dropped a pants size. She could finally see her progress when she looked in the mirror, and had even sent her aunt a full-body selfie to show off her efforts. She got a big smile and a virtual hug in return, and that encouraged her.

She had cut back drinking dramatically, and was amazed at her newfound energy. Her skin looked better, and people were commenting that she looked great.

Lastly, she sent long apologies to June, Iliana, and even Kelvin for all the things she had done to sabotage their friendship. After sending the messages on social media, she blocked each of them from her account. She did his because even though she needed to apologize, she wasn't trying to start a dialogue, and she didn't really want or need their responses.

She also called Coop, but he reassured her before she could get out her apology. "I already spoke to June," he said. "I really appreciate you doing that."

"How did she take it?"

"I think she took it well. She said she forgives you, but she doesn't think you two could ever be friends again."

"Well, I wasn't really looking for her friendship."

"I know, but that was her response."

"Right. So what about Kelvin and Iliana?"

"They both were surprised, but they were cool with it."

Camaiyah felt herself relax. "Good."

"Right."

"So... are we good?"

Coop paused. "Of course. Camaiyah, you know we family. I mean, things will be a lot easier now that that situation is over, but I would never cut you off completely. We got history."

"Right." Camaiyah sighed, relieved. "I'm glad to hear that."

After she got off the phone with Coop, she shot a quick response to Ce'Anna, who texted her while she was talking to Coop. They were supposed to be hanging out that weekend.

Camaiyah hopped in the shower then eagerly tried on her new dress, praying it fit. She bought it without trying it on in the store because she was too nervous to see how she looked under those harsh, florescent dressing room lights. So now, she took a deep breath and murmured, "Here we go." She stepped into it, did up the zipper with ease, and looked in the mirror. It was a perfect fit, and a whole size smaller than she'd been wearing for what seemed like forever!

She smiled at her reflection, posed and took a great selfie, then fixed her hair and put on some makeup. Everything had to be perfect for her date with Rashad.

**Dear Reader,**

**Ce'Anna and Camaiyah are quite the interesting duo.**

**Want to hear more about Ce'Anna's back-story, including how she lost her first husband, Trent, and ended up with Camron?**

**Check her out in A Husband, a Boyfriend, & a Side Dude.**

**Until next time,**

Tanisha Stewart

# Tanisha Stewart's Books

**Even Me Series**
Even Me
Even Me, The Sequel
Even Me, Full Circle

**When Things Go Series**
When Things Go Left
When Things Get Real
When Things Go Right

**For My Good Series**
For My Good: The Prequel
For My Good: My Baby Daddy Ain't Ish
For My Good: I Waited, He Cheated
For My Good: Torn Between The Two
For My Good: You Broke My Trust
For My Good: Better or Worse
For My Good: Love and Respect
Rick and Sharmeka: A BWWM Romance

**Betrayed Series**
Betrayed By My So-Called Friend
Betrayed By My So-Called Friend, Part 2
Betrayed 3: Camaiyah's Redemption
Betrayed Series: Special Edition
*Spin-offs coming soon!

## Phate Series
Phate: An Enemies to Lovers Romance
Phate 2: An Enemies to Lovers Romance
Leisha & Manuel: Love After Pain

## The Real Ones Series
Find You A Real One: A Friends to Lovers Romance
Find You A Real One 2: A Friends to Lovers Romance
Janie & E: Life Lessons

## Standalones
A Husband, A Boyfriend, & a Side Dude
In Love With My Uber Driver
You Left Me At The Altar
Where. Is. Haseem?! A Romantic-Suspense Comedy
Caught Up With The 'Rona: An Urban Sci-Fi Thriller
#DOLO: An Awkward, Non-Romantic Journey Through Singlehood
December 21st: An Urban Supernatural Suspense
Should Have Thought Twice: A Psychological Thriller
Everybody Ain't Your Friend
The Maintenance Man

Made in the USA
Middletown, DE
04 September 2022

73139678R00059